A Note to Parents

Your child is beginning the lifelong adventure of reading! And with the **World of Reading** program, you can be sure that he or she is receiving the encouragement needed to become a confident, independent reader. This program is specially designed to encourage your child to enjoy reading at every level by combining exciting, easy-to-read stories featuring favorite characters with colorful art that brings the magic to life.

The **World of Reading** program is divided into four levels so that children at any stage can enjoy a successful reading experience:

Reader-in-Training
Pre-K–Kindergarten
Picture reading and word repetition for children who are getting ready to read.

Beginner Reader
Pre-K–Grade 1
Simple stories and easy-to-sound-out words for children who are just learning to read.

Junior Reader
Kindergarten–Grade 2
Slightly longer stories and more varied sentences perfect for children who are reading with the help of a parent.

Super Reader
Grade 1–Grade 3
Encourages independent reading with rich story lines and wide vocabulary that's just right for children who are reading on their own.

Learning to read is a once-in-a-lifetime adventure, and with **World of Reading**, the journey is just beginning!

Printed in the United States of America
First Edition
10 9 8 7 6 5 4 3 2 1
J689-1817-1-12032
Library of Congress Control Number: 2011937891

ISBN 978-1-4231-4908-8

For more Disney Press fun, visit www.disneybooks.com
Visit DisneyChannel.com

DISNEP

Phineas and Ferb

Lost at Sea

Adapted by Leigh Stephens
Based on the series created by Dan Povenmire & Jeff "Swampy" Marsh

DISNEP PRESS
New York

One afternoon, Phineas and Ferb went sailing with their parents and their sister, Candace. Their friend Isabella came, too. They boarded the sailboat and put on their life jackets.

The boys' dad told them all about the different parts of the boat.

"Which side has the restroom?" asked Isabella.

"It's called the poop deck!" said Phineas.

"Well, no," replied Phineas's dad. He explained that the bathroom on a boat was actually called the head.

"Poop deck makes much more sense," Phineas said.

A short while later, the family boat was sailing on the ocean! Phineas saw flags in the water. He asked Isabella what they meant.

She checked her Fireside Girls handbook for the answer.

"The blue flag means crab season," she explained. "And the yellow flag means hold the mustard."

The last flag was red with a black square.

"Storm warning!" cried Isabella.

All of a sudden, the sky got dark.
"Who turned off the sun?"
Candace asked.
It started to rain. Waves crashed
over the ship, and lightning flashed
in the sky.

The sailboat was stuck in a bad storm. Before Phineas and Ferb's dad could steer the boat away, it was tossed into a large whirlpool!

When the storm cleared, the boat had crashed onto a rock by an island.

"Kids, are you all right?" Phineas and Ferb's dad asked.

"We're fine," Phineas answered.

But Candace had an octopus stuck on her head! "Hey, what gives?" she shouted. She tried to pull it off.

10

Their dad looked at the boat. It had a big hole in one side. "Mom and I will fix it," he said. "Candace, why don't you look for some food? And boys, you could find us shelter. We may be here for a while."

"You mean we're stranded?" Candace asked her mom and dad. "We'll be stuck here forever eating rocks and bugs! I'll have to marry a monkey and have monkey kids!"

Candace was upset, but Phineas and
Ferb weren't worried. They looked for
shelter along with Isabella. Soon, they
found a patch of palm trees.

"This spot has potential," Phineas said.

"Let's get started," Isabella replied.

Phineas drew plans in the sand.

Ferb cut branches.

A snake helped Isabella paint.

Together, they built a big tree house!

Meanwhile, back at home, Phineas and Ferb's pet platypus, Perry, was in the backyard.

The boys' friends Baljeet and Buford were watching the platypus while the family was away.

Baljeet and Buford didn't know that
Perry was a secret agent!

Suddenly, Perry got an urgent call
on his secret-agent wristwatch. His boss,
Major Monogram, needed his help.

But the platypus couldn't get away
without the boys seeing him.

He used the camera on his watch to
show Major Monogram what was
happening.

There was only one choice. Major Monogram had to send Carl the intern to help Perry escape.

Carl pretended to be an ice-cream-truck driver. He headed to where Baljeet and Buford were watching Perry.

"Oh, boy, ice cream!" the friends cried.

While Baljeet and Buford ordered
treats, Perry sneaked into the truck.
He put on his secret-agent hat.

"Glad to have you back, Agent P,"
Carl said. Then they zoomed away.

Major Monogram told Agent P that he needed to find Dr. Doofenshmirtz. The evil doctor was planning a new scheme. And he was on the same island as Phineas and Ferb! It was up to Agent P to stop him.

The platypus climbed onto a jet shaped like an ice-cream cone. He flew all the way to the desert island.

When he reached the island, Agent P landed inside a volcano. Dr. Doofenshmirtz was there. Agent P surprised him.

"Ahh! Perry the Platypus!" Dr. Doofenshmirtz cried. "I had a trap for you, but—no time." He pulled the platypus over to a movie screen he had set up.

Dr. Doofenshmirtz used a film to explain his evil plan to Agent P.

"Do you remember a few schemes ago when I couldn't figure out what 'Big Laundry' meant?" he asked the platypus. "Well, *this* is what I meant!"

He pointed to the screen.

"I am planning to provide the entire
Tri-State Area with free laundry!"
he cried.

By doing everyone's laundry for free, Dr. Doofenshmirtz knew that all the laundromats in the Tri-State Area would need to shut down. He planned to use the empty buildings to start his own schools of evil. Then he would have lots of students to help him with his schemes!

"I'm here on this deserted island because I get all this free monkey labor!" Dr. Doofenshmirtz explained.

He showed Agent P how he forced the monkeys on the island to do all the laundry for him.

"I control them all!" He laughed.

Agent P had to stop him!

Meanwhile, on the other side of the island, Candace saw Phineas and Ferb's tree house. It was huge!

"Can't you just be normal for one day?" she yelled. "All you had to do was make a little lean-to for survival!"

"There's survival, and then there's living!" exclaimed Phineas. "Let us give you a quick tour."

In the family room, there was a
hammock and a cozy fire.

In the kitchen, monkeys baked pies.

In the bathroom, Ferb was giving a monkey a shower.

"Had to be done," he said.

Candace was angry.

"You could have built us a bridge back to town!" she cried.

"But Dad didn't ask us to build a bridge," said Phineas.

"You could have built us a coconut-powered hovercraft!" Candace said.

"But Dad didn't ask us to," Phineas answered.

Candace stormed out, but she used
the wrong door.

"Not that way!" shouted Phineas.

Candace fell into a mud puddle.

"You two are going to be so busted!"
she yelled. She went to get her parents.

Back inside the volcano, Agent P
was fighting with Dr. Doofenshmirtz.
He hit the evil doctor with a towel.

Then Agent P kicked him into a
laundry bin on a conveyor belt.

As they fought, Dr. Doofenshmirtz
and Agent P both got tangled in the
clothes. They accidentally fell into a
tuxedo and a wedding dress!

The bin took Dr. Doofenshmirtz up to his giant washing machine and dumped him inside!

The monkeys wanted to help
Agent P defeat the evil doctor.
They threw laundry and soap into
the machine.

The clothes landed on Dr. Doofenshmirtz.
"Wait, what are you doing?" he shouted.

The monkeys poured in extra suds.
"That's too much soap!" the doctor cried.

Then they pressed the "start" button.
The washing machine rumbled. It
spun and shook. Soapsuds bubbled
out and over the top!

The monkeys screeched and ran away.

Dr. Doofenshmirtz's evil laundry plan was ruined! Quickly, Agent P jumped onto an ironing board. He used it to surf away from the volcano.

On the other side of the island, Isabella was standing on the tree house balcony. She saw the suds and thought it was lava.

"Volcano!" she yelled to Phineas and Ferb. "We need to move now!"

The friends made it out of the tree
house just in time. The pink soapsuds
spread across the island. They knocked
the giant tree house down.

Phineas, Ferb, and Isabella passed Candace.

"Run!" warned Phineas. "Pink lava behind you!"

Candace turned and saw the suds. She screamed. Then she ran, too.

On the shore, Phineas and Ferb's
parents had finished fixing the boat.
But it was still stuck on a rock.

"How are we going to get it back
in the water?" their mom asked.

Just then, the kids ran onto the beach. The pink soapsuds were right behind them!

"Mom! Dad!" cried Candace. "We've got to get out of here!"

"Hurry up, kids!" cried their dad. "Women and children first." They all climbed the ladder to the boat.

The wave of soapsuds pushed
the boat off the rock. It hit the water
and began to sail.

"Kids, we're headed home!" their dad
said happily.

No one noticed that Agent P used his surfboard to catch a ride on the back of the boat. Now that Dr. Doofenshmirtz's plan had been stopped, it was time for Agent P to head home.

Back at Phineas and Ferb's house, Baljeet was worried. Perry was missing. He used a baseball cap and a frozen waffle to make a fake Perry.

But he was pretty sure Phineas and Ferb would know the difference.

"We will have to tell them the truth!" Baljeet cried.

Soon, Phineas and Ferb arrived home. "Wait until you hear what we did today," Phineas said.

"I have something to tell you first," Baljeet said sadly.

Just then, Perry walked by. Baljeet couldn't believe his eyes!

"Thanks, Baljeet," Phineas said, smiling. "I knew we could count on you."